Victoria Wickell-Stewart

The Mouse With Wheels in His Head

**BookWilde
Children's Books**

The Mouse With Wheels in His Head

ISBN-13: 978-1482562279 / ISBN-10: 1482562278

Copyright ©2013. Second printing with Createspace Independent Publishing Platform, on white paper, laminated cover, perfect binding.

ISBN 978-1-4507-5375-3

Copyright ©2011. First printed in Bellingham, WA on heavy cream paper, stapled binding, matt cover.

Illustrated by Victoria Wickell-Stewart

Printed in the United States

All inquiries should be addressed to

BookWilde Children's Books

422 Williamson Rd.

Sequim, WA 98382

www.genegbradbury.com

This Adventure Is Dedicated

To Debbie, my companion in adventure these forty years.
To Craig and Hannah, who like Fergus, always embrace life.

~ Gene G. Bradbury

To Jim who always encouraged unconditionally.
To Jeanette and Andy who were there
through the best and worst of times
to show me that my art was what really mattered.

~ Victoria Wickell-Stewart

Long ago at the top of a house in the White City,
Fergus dreamed of machines with wheels.

"Mice cannot be engineers," said his mother.

"Why not?" asked Fergus.

"Fergus, mice cannot go to engineering school."

"But Mother," said Fergus. "Mr. Ferris is building a Ferris Wheel."

"Mr. Ferris is not a mouse," said his mother. "People are saying that Mr. Ferris has wheels in his head."

EXTRA EXTRA

FIRST MOUSE TO RIDE THE WHEEL

COLUMBIAN EXPOSITION OPENS TO CROWDS OF THOUSANDS CHICAGO.

CHICAGO. FERGUS MOUSE JOINED HUNDREDS of OTHER RIDERS on MR FERRIS' Revolutionary Wheel. PLUCKY RODENT SNEAKED ABROAD ALL ALONE!

FERGUS MOUSE HIGH ATOP MR. FERRIS' WHEEL

IN OTHER NEWS

— WEATHER —

Fergus's mother put her paws on her hips. "That's enough about wheels," she said.

"If I can't be an engineer," said Fergus, "then I must be the first mouse to ride Mr. Ferris's Wheel."

"The Wheel is made for people. It's no place for a mouse," said his mother.

Fergus imagined himself riding up, up, up,
to the very top of the world.

Every day Fergus, his father, his sister and brothers
watched the fair from the roof-top.

At night they argued about Mr. Ferris's Wheel.

"I wouldn't ride that monster," said Scruffy.

"The Wheel will get stuck," said Rosie.

"People will be too afraid to ride," said Otto.

On the opening day of the fair, Fergus watched people pass his house. Officials boarded carriages for the grand entry into the Midway.

The wheels in Fergus's head began to spin.

That night Fergus
tiptoed onto the roof.

With the fair closed, it
would be safe to explore.

Fergus climbed down the waterspout.
He scurried to the fairground and hid behind a barrel.

The guard's booth glowed from Mr. Edison's new light bulbs.
Fergus sucked in his breath when he saw the guard at the gate.
He peeked around the barrel. A shadow crept his way and growled.
Fergus stared up at a large black nose.

"Come, Masher," shouted the guard and pulled the dark shadow
down the Midway.

Fergus ran along the Avenue of Nations and past Indian Village. He hurried by Captive Balloon Park.

Fergus scooted around a building and froze.

His eyes followed the giant pillars stretching into the sky.

Mr. Ferris's Wheel was 264 feet high.

Fergus just had to be on the first ride.

How could he get aboard without being seen?

The next morning Fergus searched the newspaper.

"Mr. Ferris's Wheel opens tomorrow!" he shouted.

He stared at a picture of the marching band.

Fergus raised his eyes from the paper.

"That's how I will do it!" said Fergus.

That night Fergus opened his backpack. He placed crackers, cheese, and a bottle of water inside.

He added binoculars, ear-muffs, and a ball of soft clay. Last of all he put in a scarf and three pebbles.

Fergus slid down the waterspout and hiked to the Midway.

Fergus scurried across the street and jogged to Ferris Wheel Park.

He turned the corner and saw Masher on the speaker's platform.

The dog howled before Fergus could hide.

Masher sprang!

Fergus darted through Masher's legs and slipped
under the platform. He squeezed into a dark corner.

Masher sniffed his way along the grass.

"Masher!" the guard called.

Fergus held his breath. The dog was gone.

With heart pounding, he unrolled his sleeping bag
and went to sleep.

The next morning Fergus found the tuba among the band instruments. But next to the tuba lay Masher.

The whistle blew to start the Wheel's engines.

The sound woke Masher. The dog turned toward Fergus.

Fergus placed a pebble in the scarf. He swung the scarf over his head and let the pebble fly.

Masher spun away, but the stone struck him on the tail. He let out a howl and sprang into the moving crowd.

Fergus darted in and out of feet.

A boot missed his tail and then…
a lady's foot sent Fergus flying.

He landed with a thump near the tuba.

Fergus pulled the clay from his pack and pressed it on his feet.

He fixed the ear-muffs over his ears and began to climb up the tuba.

The tuba player lifted the tuba into the air and moved toward the Ferris Wheel.

Fergus pulled himself
inside the tuba.

The player climbed into
the first car and puckered
his lips.

The tuba BLARED!

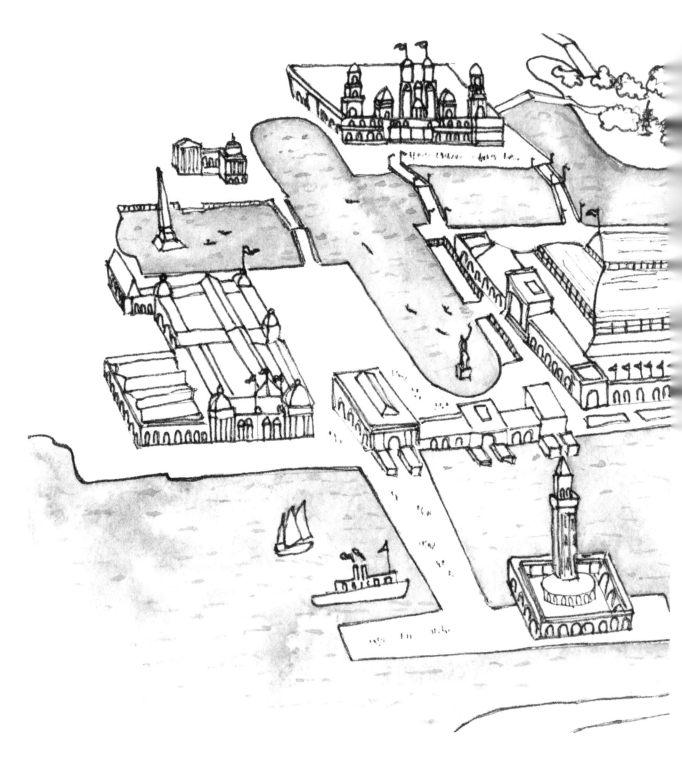

Bruised and dizzy, Fergus looked out
from the tuba's bell.

The Wheel began to move. Fergus's car reached the top.

The fairgrounds spread out below him.

Fergus raised his arms in the air. . .

"YES!" he shouted.

"I'M THE FIRST MOUSE
TO RIDE MR. FERRIS'S WHEEL!"

The End

About The First Ferris Wheel

1. The Ferris Wheel was built for the *World's Columbian Exposition* in 1893.

2. George Washington Gale Ferris invented the Wheel. He was known as *The Man with Wheels in his Head.*

3. The Ferris Wheel was 264 feet tall.

4. The Ferris Wheel took twenty minutes to make a complete revolution.

5. The first Ferris Wheel held 36 cars. Each was 24 feet long, 13 feet wide, and 10 feet high. Each could hold from 38 to 60 passengers.

6. Margaret Ferris, Mr. Ferris's wife, was the first woman to ride the Wheel.

7. The opening of Mr. Ferris's Wheel to the public was on June 21. Mr. Ferris blew a golden whistle as the signal to start the Wheel.

8. Three thousand of Mr. Edison's light bulbs blinked on and off on the Ferris Wheel.

9. The Ferris Wheel ran for four months, giving rides to 1,453,611 passengers.

BookWilde Children's Books

Visit the Author's Website:
www.genegbradbury.com

Other Books by the Author:

The Mouse Who Wanted to Fly

Adventure is in Fergus's blood. His success in riding the Ferris Wheel is in the past. When Fergus learns that two brothers, Orville and Wilbur, are going to fly the first powered airplane, Fergus is eager for a new adventure.

Is it possible that a mouse can be on the first flight at Kitty Hawk?

Mischievous Max, A Teddy Bear Story

In Leon's room you will find many teddy bears. Most of them are soft and wonderful to take to bed. But there is one bear who Leon never takes to bed. His name is Max Bear and his fur tickles and his eyes are beastly.

Leon knows something else about Max Bear. What if Leon tries sleeping with Max Bear for just one night? Would that be so bad? Leon is about to find out.

41284074R00018

Made in the USA
Charleston, SC
23 April 2015